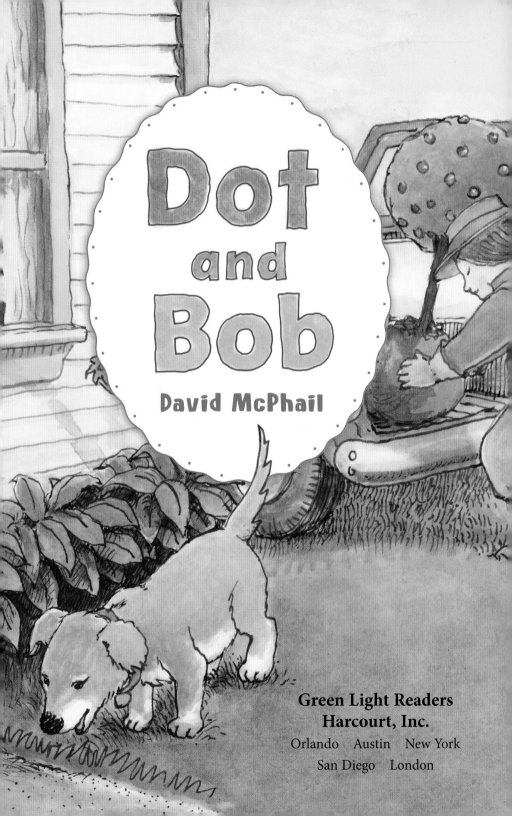

Dot and Bob

David McPhail

**Green Light Readers
Harcourt, Inc.**
Orlando   Austin   New York
San Diego   London

Bob is Dot's dog.

Bob likes to dig.

Oh, Bob! Do not dig there!

Mom has a tree.

Dot will help Mom dig.

It is hot.

It is too hot to dig.

It's not too hot for Bob!

Bob likes to dig.

Bob digs down, down, down.

Did Bob dig too much?

Mom will find out.

Look at the treetop!

Bob kicks and kicks.

Now the tree fits.

Thank you, Bob!

What Do You Think?

Who is the character
that helps Mom and Dot?

What is the problem with the hole?

Who solves the problem? How?

Do you think Bob is smart?
Why or why not?

Is Bob a good pet?
What do you like about him?
Make a list.

Meet the Author-Illustrator
David McPhail

David McPhail started drawing when he was only two years old. He would draw with a black crayon on paper bags that his grandmother cut up for him. David thought this story was fun to write and draw. "I love how the pictures help a story take shape and make sense," he says.

For information about permission to reproduce selections from this book,
please write Permissions, Houghton Mifflin Harcourt Publishing Company
215 Park Avenue South NY NY 10003.

www.hmhco.com

First Green Light Readers edition 2008

Green Light Readers and its logo are trademarks of
Houghton Mifflin Harcourt Publishing Company, registered
in the United States of America and/or other jurisdictions.

Library of Congress Cataloging-in-Publication Data
McPhail, David, 1940–
Dot and Bob/David McPhail.
p. cm.
"Green Light Readers."
Summary: When Dot's mother begins to plant a tree Bob the dog decides to help.
[1. Dogs—Fiction. 2. Pets—Fiction.] I. Title.
PZ7.M2427Do 2008
[E]—dc22   2007042338
ISBN 978-0-15-206547-8
ISBN 978-0-15-206541-6 (pb)

SCP 10 9 8
4500517275

Ages 4–6
Grade: 1
Guided Reading Level: C
Reading Recovery Level: 3

Green Light Readers
For the reader who's ready to GO!

"A must-have for any family with a beginning reader."—*Boston Sunday Herald*

"You can't go wrong with adding several copies of these terrific books to your beginning-to-read collection."—*School Library Journal*

"A winner for the beginner."—*Booklist*

Five Tips to Help Your Child Become a Great Reader

1. Get involved. Reading aloud to and with your child is just as important as encouraging your child to read independently.

2. Be curious. Ask questions about what your child is reading.

3. Make reading fun. Allow your child to pick books on subjects that interest her or him.

4. Words are everywhere—not just in books. Practice reading signs, packages, and cereal boxes with your child.

5. Set a good example. Make sure your child sees YOU reading.

Why Green Light Readers Is the Best Series for Your New Reader

● Created exclusively for beginning readers by some of the biggest and brightest names in children's books

● Reinforces the reading skills your child is learning in school

● Encourages children to read—and finish—books by themselves

● Offers extra enrichment through fun, age-appropriate activities unique to each story

● Incorporates characteristics of the Reading Recovery program used by educators

● Developed with Harcourt School Publishers and credentialed educational consultants

Look for more Green Light Readers wherever books are sold!

LEVEL 1

Buckle Up! Getting Ready to Read

simple words • fun rhymes and rhythms • familiar situations

Bob is Dot's dog, and he likes to dig!

LEVEL 1
Buckle Up!
Getting Ready to Read

LEVEL 2
Start the Engine!
Reading with Help

Developed with Harcourt School Publishers, the leader in reading education

$3.95 / Higher in Canada

ISBN 978-0-15-206541-6

5 0 3 9 5

Green Light Readers
Harcourt, Inc.
www.hmhco.com

Manufactured in China

9 780152 065416